D0931461

Hurricane Harry

by Kathryn Lay   illustrated by Jason Wolff

magic wagon

visit us at www.abdopublishing.com

To my Five-Star critique buddies, your encouragement and talent give me joy— KL

Published by Magic Wagon, a division of the ABDO Group, 8000 West 78th Street, Edina, Minnesota 55439. Copyright © 2011 by Abdo Consulting Group, Inc. International copyrights reserved in all countries. All rights reserved. No part of this book may be reproduced in any form without written permission from the publisher.

Calico Chapter Books™ is a trademark and logo of Magic Wagon.

Printed in the United States of America, Melrose Park, Illinois.
032010
092010

 This book contains at least 10% recycled materials.

Text by Kathryn Lay
Illustrations by Jason Wolff
Edited by Stephanie Hedlund and Rochelle Baltzer
Cover and interior design by Abbey Fitzgerald

Library of Congress Cataloging-in-Publication Data
Lay, Kathryn.
  Hurricane harry / by Kathryn Lay ; illustrated by Jason Wolff.
    p. cm. -- (Wendy's weather warriors ; bk. 6)
  Includes bibliographical references and index.
  ISBN 978-1-60270-759-7 (alk. paper)
  1. Hurricanes--Juvenile literature. I. Wolff, Jason, ill. II. Title.
  QC944.2.L39 2010
  551.55'2--dc22
                                    2009048841

CONTENTS

CHAPTER 1

The Big Win

Wendy ran downstairs, her arms full. Inside a bright green beach bag was her bathing suit, flip-flops, sunblock, and money for snacks at the pool.

"Bring in the mail!" her mother shouted from the kitchen.

"Okay, Mom." Wendy ducked past her dog, Cumulus, who sniffed her beach bag. She stepped onto the porch and pulled a handful of mail out of the box.

She shoved it into her mother's hand. "I'm going to wait for Jessica outside."

Wendy patted Cumulus's curly-haired head and went back outside. She and her

Weather Warrior buddies had been swimming almost every day since school let out. It was just two weeks until the new school year started.

The Warriors were all going to the new school, Cyclone Middle School, where Mr. Andrews would be the new vice principal. And thanks to the man they had helped rescue from the flash flood, there would be a new weather lab at the school. Wendy wondered how many other kids were excited about starting school again.

"Wendy," said her mom as she stepped onto the front porch, "you have mail."

Wendy clapped her hands. She had sent off for lots of information about weather. Maybe this was one of the packets.

She took the envelope and traced her fingers over her name, typed neatly. It read, Miss Wendy Peters. She didn't recognize the return address.

Wendy tore open the envelope and pulled out a piece of paper. She read the letter. Then she read it again. By the time she'd finished reading it for the third time, she was screaming. "Mom, Mom! I won! I won!"

"Won what?" Wendy's mom asked.

Wendy shook the piece of paper. "I won the big essay contest. Remember? Mr. Andrews told us about it in class at the end of the year. We had to write about an interesting event in Texas history."

She held the paper against her heart. "Of course, I wrote about the big hurricane in Galveston in 1900. It was a horrible hurricane that almost destroyed the island and killed lots of people. Remember when we went there on

vacation two years ago? Dad and I watched that video about it."

Her mother smiled. "I'm very proud of you. What's the prize?"

Wendy clapped her hands. "I get to go to Galveston on a plane. And I get to bring three other people and a chaperone. I can take the Weather Warriors." She grabbed her mom's hand. "Please, please can I go? Please talk to Dad."

Her mother squeezed Wendy's hand. "We'll discuss it."

Wendy couldn't wait to tell the Weather Warriors that they were going to go to Galveston for three days. It was a great way to end the summer.

She knew who she wanted to go as their chaperone. She hoped Mr. Andrews could get away from the new school for three days. It was going to be an amazing trip for the Weather Warriors, and Mr. Andrews had to be a part of it.

CHAPTER 2

The Big News

Wendy paced back and forth in the weather clubhouse. When she and her dad had fixed up the old clubhouse, she never dreamed she'd have a weather club and friends who loved weather as much as she did.

The clubhouse was filled with lots of new things. There was a table full of weather experiments from Dennis Galloway and photographs of their amazing weather adventures that Jessica Roberts had taken.

Even Austin Scott had started a notebook about interesting weather things he found on the Internet. He had stories of people who'd been hit by lightning more than once and survived. There were also pictures of amazing flood rescues. Austin chose anything full of excitement.

"Where is everyone?" Wendy asked Cumulus. He licked the corner of her glasses. She pulled them off her nose and wiped away the dog slobber.

"Never fear, Super Weather Scientist is here!" Dennis leaped into the room and folded his arms like a superhero wearing a stuffed backpack with glow-in-the-dark clouds all over it. "So what's the emergency?"

Wendy grinned. "You'll find out when everyone gets here."

Dennis pulled out a handful of dog treats. Cumulus danced around him.

A flash lit up the room. "Great shot," Jessica said. She stared at the screen of her digital camera and frowned. "Rats. It's too blurry."

Wendy gave her best friend a hug. "Just wait till you hear what happened."

Jessica's eyes opened wide. "What?"

Wendy just smiled.

The door to the clubhouse burst open. Austin spun into the room. "Hey, I'm a tornado." He shouted, "Kaboom! I'm thunder." He snapped his fingers over Wendy's head. "I'm pieces of hail falling on you!"

"You're weird," Wendy said.

Dennis grabbed Austin by the arm and led him to one of the chairs around the card table in the middle of the room.

"Okay Wendy, we're all here. What's this big surprise?" Dennis asked.

Wendy shook her head. "We're not all here yet. There's one more person we have to wait for."

"One more?" Jessica asked.

Someone knocked. Wendy clapped her hands when she saw Mr. Andrews standing at the door.

"Come in!" she shouted.

Mr. Andrews stepped inside. He looked around the clubhouse, nodding and smiling. "This is really amazing."

Jessica grabbed her camera and took a picture of their fifth grade teacher. "We haven't seen you all summer," she said.

Dennis shook Mr. Andrews's hand. Wendy giggled.

"So, what's this big, important meeting about?" Mr. Andrews asked.

Wendy took a deep breath. "The big announcement is: I won the Texas history essay contest you told us about! I won a trip to the coast—to Galveston Island—for three days next week, and you're all invited to go with me."

Wendy had never heard it so quiet in the clubhouse. She held her breath and waited. Maybe they didn't want to go. Maybe they couldn't go.

Dennis started the first cheer. Then everyone was hugging Wendy and talking all at once about the trip.

Wendy snapped her fingers. The Weather Warriors were going mobile.

CHAPTER 3

The First Plane Ride

Wendy pulled her luggage in a circle. She watched other passengers as they walked quickly back and forth, looking for their own flights.

"Is it time for our plane yet?" Jessica asked. She took pictures of everyone together, of each of them separate, of the sign for their gate number, and lots of pictures of the planes outside the windows. She even took pictures of the little restaurant where they each had a sandwich.

Wendy checked her watch again. Then she walked up to the man standing behind the little counter. "Is our plane ready?"

He shook his head. "Like I said before, when they are ready for you to board, we'll announce it."

Wendy ran back to the others. They had said good-bye to their parents at the security checkpoint. Her mother cried a little. It would be Wendy's first plane ride. Austin and Jessica had flown before, but Wendy and Dennis were on a new adventure.

Mr. Andrews stared outside at the plane. "I wonder if that's ours. It doesn't look very big, does it? But it's a short flight, isn't that what they said?"

Wendy nodded. Mr. Andrews was acting strange.

"We are now boarding for flight 4368 to Houston," the man at the counter announced.

"Whee!" Austin shouted. "That's us."

Wendy grinned. It felt like butterflies were tap dancing in her stomach. She looked at Mr. Andrews. His face looked pale and his hands shook. Wendy nudged Jessica.

"Mr. Andrews, are you sick?" Jessica asked.

He tugged at his ponytail. He tapped his nose. He cleared his throat. "Well, uh, you see . . . I've never been on a plane either."

Wendy said, "Oh." She figured an adult his age must have been on a plane at least once.

"The three of us can sit together and be the first-time-on-a-plane club," Dennis said.

They all followed Austin to the line of people waiting to show the gate agent their tickets. As they walked through the tunnel to the plane, Austin hopped in front of them and shouted "Ribbit!"

Wendy's heart pounded when she stepped into the plane. There were three seats on one side of the plane and two on the other. She switched seats with Jessica so that she, Dennis, and Mr. Andrews were sitting together.

Once their carry-on luggage was put into the overhead compartment, they sat in their seats and talked about what they would do in Galveston.

"We have to go to the museum about the 1900 Hurricane at five o'clock," Wendy said. "They are having a party for me, and I get to read my essay."

"Cool!" Jessica said, leaning across the aisle. "What else is there to do in Galveston? I've never been there before."

Wendy held up her hand and touched each finger as she said, "There is Moody Gardens that has these cool glass pyramids with an aquarium and rain forest and 3-D movies. And the beach, of course. And a miniature golf course on a hill across from the ocean. And lots of pelicans and seagulls you can take pictures of and . . ."

"And sharks?" Austin asked.

Wendy shivered. "I hope not."

A voice over the intercom said, "Hello, this is your pilot and we're about to taxi onto the runway. We'll be taking off a few moments after that. Turn off your cell phones please, and make sure your seat belts are buckled."

Wendy could hear the clicks as everyone fastened their seat belts. She took a deep breath as the plane began to move. Mr. Andrews gave a nervous laugh. He joked, "Well, guess it's too late to get off now."

Wendy nodded. "This is going to be fun. My dad flies all the time for his job."

Suddenly, the plane moved faster. Wendy grabbed the arms of her seat. She closed her eyes as she felt the plane leave

the ground. An invisible hand pushed her back against her seat.

"G-force!" Jessica said from across the aisle.

Wendy nodded, but kept her eyes closed as the plane move upward.

"Everything looks small," Dennis said.

Wendy opened one eye. Dennis had his face pressed against the window. Mr. Andrews had his eyes closed tight. Wendy's stomach seemed to float a minute as the plane climbed higher and higher, then turned and leveled off.

They were on their way. And soon, she would be giving a speech about weather. A speech to a lot of strangers. Even though the plane was moving smoothly, her stomach began to do a butterfly dance again.

CHAPTER 4

Who's Harry?

Wendy sat in the front seat of the van Mr. Andrews had rented at the airport in Houston. She was glad they were on the ground again. They had been driving for longer than they flew.

"There's Galveston Bay!" she said. "On the other side of that bridge, we'll be in Galveston."

"Cool bridge," Jessica said. She pressed her camera against the window and snapped pictures. Soon, they were crossing over the bay to where the houses sat on stilts.

"Wow, look at the pelicans!" Austin shouted, pointing to the large brown birds sitting at the edge of the docks. "I thought they were pink."

Dennis gave Austin a shove. "That's flamingos. Pelicans are brown or white."

Wendy rolled down her window and breathed in the fishy, salty smell of the water.

"I have this experiment where you can separate the salt out of salt water," Dennis said. He pulled out his notebook full of experiments and tapped it. "Maybe I could tell people about it when you read your essay."

Wendy shrugged. "It's at a museum about the hurricane from the year 1900. And my essay is about the hurricane."

Dennis tapped the notebook against his nose. "Hmm. I don't have any hurricane experiments."

Mr. Andrews said, "Okay everyone, we're officially in Galveston."

Wendy and the others clapped and cheered. Wendy could see the deep blue glass pyramid of the aquarium at Moody Gardens and the clear one of the rain forest.

"We'll check in at the hotel first," Mr. Andrews said. "Then we'll go to the museum and let them know we're here. The celebration for your winning essay is in five hours, Wendy."

Wendy caught her breath. Now that it was almost time, she wondered how she would stand up in front of strangers and read. What if lots of people came? What if she read too quiet or stumbled over the words and sounded silly?

"Wow!" Dennis shouted. "There's the ocean!"

Mr. Andrews stopped the van at a light. In front of them was the beach and the Gulf of Mexico. They turned and drove along a road that ran right beside the beach.

"What's that big wall thing?" Jessica asked.

Mr. Andrews said, "It's the seawall. It helps keep the storm surge from flooding the city during a tropical storm or hurricane."

Wendy nodded. "It was built after the big hurricane I wrote about. That's why this road is called Seawall Boulevard. And there are cool paintings on the wall and some sculptures, too."

They stopped at a hotel across from the beach.

"Here we are," Mr. Andrews said. "Our home for the next three days."

The group piled out of the van and into the hotel lobby. Austin ran over to the racks of colorful brochures that told about things to do. Jessica took pictures of the lobby, the hotel workers, and the ocean scene out the windows. Dennis ran to the computers against the wall.

Wendy followed Mr. Andrews to the front desk.

"We have two adjoining room reservations," Mr. Andrews said.

Wendy waved at the woman behind the desk. "My name is Wendy, and I'm the winner of the essay contest."

The woman smiled and nodded. "Oh yes, we've been expecting your group Miss Peters." She turned to Mr. Andrews. "Are you their chaperone?"

When he nodded, the woman said, "Please fill out this form and include everyone's name. Your room will be ready in about four hours if you'd like to look around town."

Dennis frowned. "You mean we can't go see our room?"

Mr. Andrews shook his head. "We're here a bit early for check-in time. But we can have some lunch and go over to the bay side where the museums are. Then, we'll go to the party for Wendy."

Austin held up a brochure. "Hey, there's a film about a pirate in Galveston!"

Dennis grabbed it. "No kidding?"

Wendy nodded. "Yep, Jean Lafitte. It's at the same place as the Great Storm film."

They hurried back to the van and drove to the other side of the island, where the piers held shrimp boats and lots of restaurants. They watched the shrimpers moving in and out of the bay. They parked and got directions to the museum where Wendy would be speaking.

"Look at that boat!" Austin shouted.

"It's a sailing ship," Mr. Andrews said. "The *Elissa*. It says on this plaque that it's from 1877. They also call it the tall ship Elissa."

They stared at the ship docked beside the museum.

"Hey, we can take a tour of it," Austin said, waving another brochure.

They bought tickets to tour the ship. They walked around the deck and climbed below to where the sailors would sleep. Austin jumped around and around until Mr. Andrews agreed they could go see the film about the pirate Jean Lafitte.

Wendy thought the pirate film was interesting. But she couldn't stop thinking about reading her essay to strangers.

After the film, they looked through the shops on the Strand and ate lunch at a hamburger restaurant where the tables were outside. They took turns getting their picture taken in front of a big wall at the restaurant where water flowed down.

Mr. Andrews said, "We need to get back to the Great Storm Theater. The celebration for Wendy will start soon."

He looked at Wendy and smiled. "You're going to take them by storm."

Wendy nodded and tried to swallow the last bite of hamburger as she heard a radio in the restaurant. She caught the words *tropical storm*. The voice talked about someone named Harry.

She walked over to the radio sitting beside the cash register. "Can I help you?" a woman at the register asked.

Wendy nodded. "Who's Harry?"

The waitress said, "Oh yes, tropical storm Harry. He's out in the Gulf. Could be heading our way, but I wouldn't worry."

Wendy thanked her and sat back down with her friends. She wondered if she should mention the storm to them. Sometimes a tropical storm would cross Mexico and then get stronger in the warm waters of the Gulf of Mexico. What if Harry did that? Would they be in the path of the storm? Could it become a hurricane?

She had read enough about the 1900 hurricane to know she didn't want to be caught in one. Even a smaller hurricane sounded scary.

CHAPTER 5

Hurricanes Old and New

"Stop taking my picture," Wendy said.

Jessica grinned and turned to take pictures of the room where a crowd of people were already finding seats. A banner hung on the wall to welcome Wendy and balloons floated around the room. The podium stood in front of the screen where the film about the 1900 Hurricane was shown once every hour.

"I think I wish no one would have come," Wendy whispered.

Jessica shook her head. "No you don't. You did a great job on the essay and lots of people want to hear it. And after this is all over, we have two more days to look at all the sights."

Wendy nodded. It sounded exciting. But now, she couldn't think about anything else but reading her essay.

Mr. Andrews and a woman in a red suit walked over to them. The woman smiled at Wendy and held out her hand.

"Hello, Wendy. I'm Mrs. Moore. I'm in charge of the Fifth Grade Texas History Essay Project. I just want to say how much I enjoyed your essay on the hurricane. It was very well thought out."

Wendy shook the woman's hand. "I love to learn about weather."

Mr. Andrews said, "I've been telling Mrs. Moore about the Weather Warriors and your amazing weather station. I told her about all the ways you've helped the school and even rescued people this past year during different kinds of weather."

Dennis and Austin ran up to the group. "Wow, did you see your picture by the door?" Dennis said.

Wendy nodded. Her mom had helped her pick out a good photograph to send. She wished she had found one without her glasses.

Mrs. Moore said, "We have a wonderful crowd. There are teachers from the local schools and that's the mayor sitting over there. The city of Galveston is very honored that the winner of the contest wrote about something in their history."

Suddenly, the mayor stood from the front row and walked to the podium. She leaned into the microphone. "Welcome everyone, and please take your seats. We are honored today to have some young visitors to our island. In particular, one young lady who will read her winning essay.

"After the reading, we'll watch the film about the 1900 Hurricane. Then there will be refreshments in the back to give you time to meet Wendy and her friends.

"One quick note, most of you have probably heard that there is a tropical storm heading toward the coast. It may hit here or farther up the coast toward Louisiana and just bring us some rain. But we all know how quickly weather can change, so be aware of what's going on."

She motioned toward Wendy. "Now, I'd like Miss Wendy Peters to step up here."

Everyone applauded as Wendy walked to the front of the room. She shook hands with the mayor. After the mayor sat down, Wendy pulled a folded piece of paper

from her pocket. She smoothed it out on the podium.

"Uh, hello. My name is Wendy, and I love to learn about weather. My friends with me are part of the Wendy's Weather Warriors club. And that man with them was our teacher." She took a deep breath and began to read.

"On September 8, 1900, on Galveston Island, on the coast of Texas, a hurricane like no other hit the city. When it was over, there were at least 6,000 people who died. The storm left the city in ruins.

"Before the storm, Galveston had grown from a small settlement into one of the wealthiest cities in the country. Seventy percent of our country's cotton crop was exported through Galveston's port and people came from all over to vacation on the island."

Wendy peered over her paper at the crowd. They were nodding and watching her. She took another deep breath and spoke louder. "But then the hurricane came ashore and washed through the streets. It knocked down houses, even when people were inside. Lots of people were swept out with the water. I think it is very sad that this happened to Galveston."

She read about the seawall and how it was built so such a terrible thing might not happen again. She talked about how people helped each other and rescued people around them.

"Historical places like the Moody Mansion survived the storm and were restored."

Then with a solemn expression she said, "I love Galveston. It is beautiful and fun and has lots of nice people. I hope there is never something as bad as the 1900 Hurricane there ever again. And I am glad we now have people who fly into hurricanes to learn about them and that there are warnings to let people know when to leave."

She folded her paper and said, "Thank you for letting me and my friends come."

Austin jumped up and led the applause. Afterward, many people came to shake Wendy's hand. Mrs. Moore led her to the back of the room where there were sandwiches, fruit, and brownies.

"You did great," Jessica said, snapping a picture of Wendy with her plate of food. "I took lots of pictures of you reading your essay. I even got one of you and the mayor shaking hands!"

Wendy grinned. "I'm glad it's over. That was scary. But it was fun, too."

She opened her mouth to take a bite of a strawberry when she heard the microphone squeal behind her.

"Can I have your attention please? It's strange I should be making this announcement right now, but it appears that the storm is not going to make landfall near Beaumont. It should arrive here sometime tomorrow."

Wendy looked at her friends. Her heart pounded. This was their chance to see what it was like being in a tropical storm.

The mayor tapped the microphone again. "The weather service says that with the slow forward motion of the storm, it could become a category 1 hurricane. So please, be aware and listen to your radio and television."

"A hurricane!" Dennis said. "I need to make some notes for a hurricane experiment."

Austin weaved back and forth, knocking into the Weather Warriors.

"Whoosh, I'm a windy hurricane coming to get you."

Jessica giggled and took his picture. Wendy frowned. How could her friends act like it was just a game after hearing her essay? They needed a safety plan.

She hurried across the room to find Mr. Andrews.

CHAPTER 6

Shelter

At breakfast the next morning, Wendy and Jessica looked out the restaurant window.

"There sure are lots more clouds out there now," Jessica said.

Wendy agreed. "The wind is stronger, too. See how much higher the waves are? And it smelled like salty rain in the air when we walked outside the hotel."

"I want to go to the aquarium," Austin announced. He stuffed a pancake in his mouth and mumbled, "I bet they have sharks."

Wendy pointed out the window. "If that storm does come in and it becomes a hurricane, I don't think I want to be inside a giant glass pyramid."

Mr. Andrews was standing by the cash register, talking on his cell phone. Wendy had a feeling he was calling their parents.

After breakfast, they drove back to the hotel. Mr. Andrews went straight to the phone. Wendy and the others sat in the girls' room and watched the weather channel.

Wendy could hear Mr. Andrews talking with the airlines about getting a flight home sooner. She hated to leave early and she knew her friends were upset with her for suggesting it. Wendy just wasn't sure they should stay and take a chance being caught in a tropical storm, or maybe even a small hurricane?

She walked onto the balcony. The hotel was shaped like a V and every balcony faced toward the ocean. The waves were high. There were surfers riding on the waves and lots of people still walking on the beach. They didn't seem worried.

Dennis stood beside her. "Those waves look awesome."

Wendy shrugged. "I guess. They're getting really rough. Look at those white caps. But, it's still crowded around here. Maybe it's no big deal."

Dennis clapped her on the back. "Yeah, it'll probably be over before we know it and then we can finish our trip. You're just spooked after reading that essay and seeing the film and those pictures from the big storm."

"Listen everyone," Mr. Andrews said. "I called the local radio station. The storm has picked up speed. It looks like it'll be a category 1 hurricane when it hits.

"Houston has grounded planes coming in and out until it's over. We can drive farther inland or ride it out here. If it gets worse than they think, I don't want to stay at this hotel on the beach. I found out the high school is closer to the middle of the island and it's set up as a shelter."

Austin jumped up on the couch and pretended to surf. "Cool! We're going to ride the storm."

Wendy frowned. What did Austin know about hurricanes? They had only let him in the Weather Warriors because of his dad's snow machine. But even her friends, who loved to learn about weather and weather safety, didn't want to leave.

"I guess I'm just a worrywart like Dad calls my grandma," she mumbled.

Jessica said, "I'd love to get some pictures of a hurricane to add to my collection. We could hang one at the clubhouse next to your certificate for winning the essay contest," she suggested.

Wendy said, "A hurricane is wind and flooding rain mostly. Lots of it. Not sure if you will get any good pictures." She turned to Mr. Andrews, "I think it's a good idea to try to pack up and drive now. It can be dangerous once the storm moves inland."

As if reading her mind, the wind blew harder, knocking over chairs on the balcony. Seagulls flew against the wind, struggling to rise over the hotel. Wendy could see the rain out on the ocean.

The storm would hit soon.

A loud beep interrupted the television program.

"Tropical storm Harry has been officially upgraded to a category 1

hurricane. Hurricane Harry is expected to hit along the Texas gulf coast. Residents all along the coast are urged to take shelter in a sturdy building, away from windows and rising water. High winds, heavy rain, and some tornadoes are possible."

Austin's eyes went wide. He stepped off the sofa and sat down. "I want to go home," he whispered.

Wendy patted his shoulder and said, "We'll be okay."

"Why did you bring us here?" Austin said. "You're supposed to be the weather know-it-all."

Wendy shook her head. "Sometimes these storms can come up quick. Tropical Storm Allison in 2001 came up really suddenly."

She grabbed her beach bag and dumped out her bathing suit, towel, and beach shoes. "I think we should pack a few things quick and go to that school shelter."

Mr. Andrews nodded.

CHAPTER 7

What's in the Water?

"Wow, did you see that sign blow by?" Austin shouted as they piled into the van.

Wendy fought the wind to pull the van door shut. She was surprised at how fast the storm was growing. The rain blew sideways. The ocean surf beat against the seawall. There were only a few cars on the road as they pulled out of the hotel.

"I remember passing the school while we were out yesterday," Mr. Andrews said. "We're almost there. It doesn't take long to get anywhere on the island going south to north. It's longer than it is wide."

Dennis pressed his nose against the car window. "I wonder how high those winds are. I bet my anemometer would go nuts."

Wendy pulled out a little booklet from her backpack. "This tells about tropical storms and hurricanes. It says that a tropical storm with winds of 39 to 73 miles per hour becomes a hurricane when the winds near the eye get to 74 miles per hour. And listen to this, the average wind speed can get up to 74 to 95 miles an hour for a category 1 hurricane."

Jessica pointed at the way the street lights were swaying back and forth. "That's pretty fast. I hope our van doesn't blow away. And what about the hotel with all our stuff in it?"

Wendy looked through the book. "With a category 1, most of the damage is to trees and bushes. There usually isn't a lot of real damage to big buildings like hotels."

Jessica nodded. She took her camera and snapped pictures out the window. "I don't think these will be very good with the rain all over the window."

Mr. Andrews slowed the van and turned into a driveway. "We're here. See, there are people going inside the auditorium doors."

He parked the van, hopped out, and struggled to open the door. "Everyone out. Hold hands!"

Wendy grabbed Jessica's hand as they leaped into the wind and rain. She could barely see Mr. Andrews as he led them across the parking lot. The tops of the palm trees around them bent in the wind. A stop sign shook as if a giant were pulling it back and forth.

By the time they reached the school and were let inside, they were soaked.

"Ugh," Jessica said. "We should be wearing our bathing suits. It's icky being in wet clothes."

Mr. Andrews nodded as he squeezed the water from his ponytail. "That's why I told everyone to put clothes in their backpack. After we check into the shelter, we all need to change into something dry."

They stood in a line by a long table while Mr. Andrews registered them. Each of them was given an ID bracelet.

"Now, go change," Mr. Andrews ordered with a wink.

Wendy and Jessica asked a woman standing beside a coffee machine where to find the girls' bathroom.

"It's just down the hall and on your right," she said. "You girls are really soaked."

Wendy nodded. "Yes ma'am. Are there a lot of people here?"

The woman nodded. She pulled back her hair and tied it in a ponytail. "Most of the kids are in the media room next door watching a movie. You're welcome to join them. Just stay away from the pool. We'll be serving lunch soon."

They thanked the woman and ran to the bathroom.

"Yuck, I hate being in wet clothes," Jessica said, pulling bright green shorts and a T-shirt from her beach bag.

Wendy nodded. She listened to the wind howling around them. Would they be safe in the school? What if it flooded? What if their van floated away? Or the hotel with all their stuff inside was destroyed?

"I wish I had my weather radio with me," she said.

The lights flickered, then went out. Jessica screamed. Wendy stood still in the dark bathroom. After a moment, the lights went back on.

"They must have a generator," Wendy said.

After they were dressed, they hurried back to the auditorium. Someone had crisscrossed gray duct tape on the outside doors to keep the glass from breaking.

Mr. Andrews stood with Dennis and Austin. "Sure feels good to have dry clothes on again," he said. "Many of the people here are vacationers, like us, staying at the hotels along the seawall."

"How long will the storm last?" Jessica asked.

Wendy shrugged. "It could rain for a long time. For hours even."

"Maybe we'll see a shark float past," Austin said. He snapped his teeth at them and wandered over to the outside doors.

"A shark would get a stomachache if it ate him," Jessica said.

Mr. Andrews pointed to the front of the gymnasium. "Looks like they're putting out some food."

"Mmm. Hot dogs," Wendy said. She grabbed Jessica's arm. They were halfway across the gym when she heard a shout.

"Hey, there's something out there!"

Wendy turned and saw Austin pointing out the doors.

"It's swimming in the parking lot. It's coming toward us!" he yelled.

Wendy stared at Jessica. They ran over to the door. Did Austin's shark really get swept inland? Wendy looked into the wind and rain at the creature coming toward them.

CHAPTER 8

A Whimper for Help

"It's a dog!" Dennis shouted.

Wendy gasped as the small, tan dog struggled against the wind. It whimpered and barked. The water in the parking lot was up to the car tires. The dog swam through the rising waters.

"We've got to go get him," Wendy said, pushing at the glass door. It was locked. She struggled to turn the knob.

"Young lady, what are you doing?" a man shouted, running toward them.

Jessica pointed out the door. "There's a little dog caught in the storm. He'll drown or be swept away. We have to rescue him."

The man shook his head. "You can't go out there, it's too dangerous. You could be swept away, too. Or hit by debris flying in the wind."

The howl of the wind outside, even with the door closed, sounded like some giant creature trying to blow its way inside. Lawn chairs, palm fronds, and a kid's blow-up swimming pool flew past the door, caught up in the wind.

Mr. Andrews moved between Wendy and the door. "He's right. I'm sorry about the dog, but we can't go out there."

Wendy folded her arms. "Pets are lost or abandoned during hurricanes lots of times. That dog belongs to someone." Her throat felt tight. What if it was Cumulus, lost and alone in a storm like this? She'd want someone to rescue him.

Dennis pointed out the door. "He's swimming in circles. He doesn't know where to go."

Mr. Andrews shook his head. "I'm sorry. I'm responsible for you kids and your safety."

Austin pushed his way through the crowd that was gathering around the door. He held several hot dogs. He gave one to Wendy. She glared at him and shouted, "How can you think about eating when that poor little dog is out there?"

Austin waved a hot dog in her face. "When my grandma's dog ran away, we chased him and no one could catch him. Then my dad came with a package of bologna and held it out. Tiger loves bologna. He ran right over to us."

Wendy's mouth dropped open. Every time she wondered why they let Austin in their club, he surprised her and said something important.

Wendy snapped her fingers. "That's a great idea, Austin."

Austin's face turned red. He pushed past Wendy and went to the man in charge of the shelter. "We'll have to open that door just a little."

The man nodded.

He unbolted the latch and inched the door open enough for Austin to reach his hand through and throw a hot dog into the parking lot. It splashed behind the dog.

"Rats! He didn't see it," Austin said.

"Let me try," Dennis said. "My dad says I have a good throwing arm."

Dennis took a hot dog and tossed it. It landed right next to the wide-eyed dog.

The dog swam toward the hot dog and grabbed it. He chewed and swallowed.

Wendy clapped her hands. "Do it again, but make it closer to the door."

Dennis and Austin took turns throwing hot dogs. Sometimes the dog saw them and moved closer to the door, and sometimes he didn't.

Jessica snapped pictures.

Wendy watched the little dog. It looked tired. It wasn't paddling as hard, even though the water was still rising.

"I don't think he's going to make it to the door," Wendy said. She looked around the gym for something that could help them rescue the dog.

Then she remembered what the woman standing by the coffee told her and Jessica when they were looking for a bathroom. She snapped her fingers and grabbed Austin by the arm.

"Come with me! I have an idea."

CHAPTER 9

The Rescue

Wendy found the woman she talked to earlier. "Please, we need your help."

The woman was setting a tray of fruit on the table beside the hot dog buns. She looked up at Wendy and Austin. "Help yourself to the food. They say the hurricane will pass quickly, but it will be dangerous driving on the flooded roads tonight."

"We're not hungry," Wendy said. "But I need to get into the pool room. Do you know who has the keys?"

The woman raised her eyebrows. "Didn't you get wet enough before? I'm afraid there will be no swimming."

Austin stared at Wendy. "I can't swim."

Wendy sighed. "We don't want to swim. I need to get something that I'm sure is in that room. And fast. It's a matter of life or death."

The woman gasped. "What?"

Wendy explained about the stranded dog. "We can't go into the parking lot to get him and he's too tired to get to the door. But I thought if we could hook him somehow and pull him to us . . ."

The woman smiled. "Yes, I see what you mean." She reached into her pocket and pulled out a ring full of keys. "I'm the one you need to find. I'm the principal here."

Wendy and Austin followed her out the gym doors and down the hall. A big sign over a set of double doors said, "Pool

Room. No one admitted without a coach or a teacher."

The principal unlocked the door and led them inside. She pointed to a corner. "Is that what you are looking for?"

Wendy nodded. She and Austin ran over to a wall where a tall pole with a net on the end hung on a rack. Austin grabbed it.

"We've got to hurry," Wendy said.

She and Austin thanked the principal and ran back to the gym. When they got to the door, it looked like everyone at the shelter had crowded near it.

"Excuse us, please!" Wendy shouted.

She pushed through the crowd and led the way for Austin. When they got to the door, Wendy could see the dog was trying to paddle to the door. Mr. Andrews and

Dennis were whistling and calling the dog.

"Step aside!" Austin said. "I'm here to save the day."

He pushed the pole through the door opening while Mr. Andrews held onto the door to keep the wind from blowing it wide open.

"Farther to your left," Jessica suggested.

Dennis stepped behind Austin and grabbed the pole as it moved in the wind.

Austin pushed the net end of the pole closer to the dog. He swung down. The net fell onto the dog's tail.

"Keep trying," Wendy begged.

Austin raised the pole again. The wind caught it. "Aaagh!" Austin yelled. "I can't hold on!"

Wendy grabbed the end of the pole behind Dennis. Together the three of them held it against the wind.

"Move it down now!" Dennis shouted.

Wendy felt the pole move as Austin lowered it. She held on tight to it.

Suddenly everyone around them applauded.

"Pull!" Austin ordered.

Wendy pulled back. Together she, Dennis, and Austin stepped backward into the gym. Mr. Andrews opened the door a little bit wider.

"He's in!" Austin shouted.

Mr. Andrews shut the door and bolted it. Wendy fell backward as Austin let go of the pole. She jumped up when she heard a whimper.

"Is the dog okay?" she asked, crawling toward it.

The brown terrier whimpered and shivered. He gave himself a big shake and water flew all over Austin. "Hey dog, I just rescued you!"

"This is going to make a great series of photos," Jessica said. "I can see the

caption: Weather Warriors Rescue Dog From Hurricane Harry."

Someone brought a blanket and gave it to Wendy. She wrapped the little dog in the blanket and held him close.

"You poor thing," she said as the dog gave her a quick lick on the cheek. She wondered if other pets were caught out in the storm. She wondered who this dog belonged to and if they were safe somewhere.

She turned the dog's collar around. There were two tags. One was from a veterinarian clinic and one listed an address and phone number.

Wendy followed her friends to cots that were set up around the gym. She climbed into one and lay the dog down beside her. Before long, he curled in a ball against her shoulder, snoring quietly.

"That poor dog is really tired," Jessica said, bending over to give him a quick pat.

"I'm naming him Shark," Austin said. "He can sit on my lap on the plane."

Wendy stared at Austin. "He belongs to someone here. You can't keep him."

Austin folded his arms. "Says you!" He lay back on his cot and closed his eyes.

Wendy could hear the wind blowing outside. Would the storm ever end?

She rubbed the dog's wet head. If they hadn't have come to Galveston, what would have happened to him? It was worth all the work to get him safely inside.

Wendy closed her eyes and listened to the wind outside. It was beating against the walls as if it wanted to get inside, too.

CHAPTER 10

Save the Sharks . . . Uh, Pets!

"Wake up, Wendy. It's over!"

Wendy opened her eyes. Dennis was standing over her. Something cold pressed against her cheek. "The storm is over. We can leave now."

Wendy squealed as a furry puppy jumped at her. "Okay, I'm awake."

She sat up and pulled the little dog into her arms.

"They said we can leave," Dennis said. "We're going to go to the hotel and get our stuff. Then we're going home."

Wendy frowned. "Home? But we have one more day here."

She jumped off the cot. People around her were packing satchels and suitcases and leaving the school gym.

The dog followed her to the door that led outside. She opened it and squinted at the bright sun.

"Can you believe what a beautiful day it is after last night?" Jessica said. She pointed to the parking lot. "It's really messy, but nothing is destroyed except a few bushes."

Wendy looked at the debris on the ground. Dirt from trash cans had blown around. A street sign was lying in a lawn. Palm fronds were lying everywhere. Hurricane Harry was over.

Austin zoomed around Wendy. He picked up the dog. "Mr. Andrews said we could find this address and take the dog home before we drive back to the airport."

Wendy smiled. "Great. I'd sure want to see Cumulus right away."

They piled into the van. The dog sat in the seat between Austin and Wendy. Mr. Andrews followed the directions the shelter director had given him to find the dog's home.

"It's just around this corner," he said. "The dog didn't get far from home."

Austin took off his shoe, then his sock. He rolled the sock into a ball and waved it at the dog.

"Eeew," Jessica said. "Stop torturing that poor dog, Austin."

Austin crossed his eyes at her. The van stopped outside a blue house sitting high up on stilts.

"This is his home," Mr. Andrews said.

They walked up the stairs to the door and knocked. The door opened and a woman peered outside. "Yes?"

Wendy held out the dog. "I think we found your dog last night. He was caught in the storm."

The woman held out her arms. The little dog wagged its tail and whined.

"Socks! We thought you'd been swept into the gulf," the woman said. The dog leaped into her arms. She smiled at the group standing on her porch. "I can't thank you enough."

Wendy clapped her hands. "We're so glad we helped him. We're here on a trip, and we have to leave now."

The woman thanked them again. As they climbed back into the van, Austin folded his arms and said, "Socks? That's a silly name. His name should be Shark."

At the hotel, the manager gave them passes for two free nights each whenever they wanted to come back.

As they drove back through Galveston, Wendy looked at the damage that Hurricane Harry had done. None of the street lights were working. There were bushes and signs and other things in the road that they had to drive around.

"Will it be expensive to clean everything up?" she asked.

Mr. Andrews nodded. "It's always expensive after a hurricane."

"Could we help?" Jessica asked. She rolled down the van window and snapped photos of the damage around them.

Wendy snapped her fingers. "That's a great idea. We could raise money at home to send back here. Maybe to the school where the shelter was or . . ."

Austin snapped his fingers and said, "My idea is better."

Dennis leaned forward from the seat behind them. "What is it?"

Austin grinned at them, then barked.

Wendy knew what he meant. There had to be other pets that needed help after the storm. "We can send money to the animal shelter so they can help save animals that are lost or hurt by Harry."

Mr. Andrews said, "I'll be glad to help you get the word out back home. It's frightening for the animals and sad for the families when their pets are lost. We can help save cats and dogs and . . ."

Austin wiggled his eyebrows. "And sharks! Save the sharks."

Wendy giggled. Hurricane Harry might be gone, but they still had Austin around.

From the Author

This story represents the many small tropical storms and hurricanes that have hit the Texas coast over the years. But it is not meant to detract from the tragedy of Hurricane Ike, which hit Galveston and the Texas coast on September 14, 2008.

My family and I have spent many wonderful vacations in Galveston, Crystal Beach, and the Kemah Boardwalk; all areas hugely affected by Ike. My heart goes out to all those affected. But, I know that the area where my story takes place will work hard and recover again.

Hurricane Ike was the third most destructive hurricane to make landfall in the United States. This category 4 hurricane slammed into the Galveston, Houston, and surrounding coastal areas of Texas, damaging homes, businesses, and piers. Many lives were lost. Hurricane Ike went from a tropical storm to a category 4 hurricane in just hours.

The hurricane of 1900 made landfall on the city of Galveston on September 8, 1900. It had estimated winds of 135 miles per hour at landfall, making it a category 4 storm. Official reports say that there were around 6,000 deaths. The Galveston Hurricane of 1900 is the deadliest natural disaster ever to strike the United States. The most recent deadliest storm was Hurricane Katrina (approximately 1,800 deaths).

Galveston's 1900 hurricane happened before there were official code names assigned to tropical storms. Because of this, the storm has been called by many names: the Galveston Hurricane of 1900, the Great Galveston Hurricane, and, especially in older documents, the Galveston Flood. It is often referred to by Galveston locals as the Great Storm or the 1900 Storm.

Did You Know?

🌀 A hurricane is a huge storm that begins in the ocean. A hurricane can be as wide as 600 miles (1,000 km) across. The winds can get as high 200 miles per hour (300 km/h). These storms gather heat and energy because of contact with warm ocean waters.

🌀 Hurricanes rotate in a counter-clockwise direction in the northern hemisphere around the center of the storm, which is called the "eye." When a hurricane hits land, the heavy rain, strong winds, and storm surge can damage buildings, trees, and cars. It causes flooding and often creates tornadoes.

🌀 The Atlantic hurricane season is from June 1 to November 30. Most hurricanes there happen during the early fall months. The Eastern Pacific hurricane season is from May 15 to November 30.

DENNIS'S Hurricane Safety Tips

BEFORE A HURRICANE: Have a disaster plan ready. If you have pets, make sure you have a plan for them as well. You can contact your veterinarian or the local humane society for more information before a storm threatens. Board up windows and bring in outdoor objects that could blow away. Make sure you know where all the evacuation routes are.

Prepare a disaster supply kit for your home and car. The disaster kit should include a first aid kit, canned food and a can opener, enough bottled water for three days, a battery-operated radio, a flashlight, and protective clothing. Also include written instructions on how to turn off electricity, gas, and water. Have a NOAA weather radio handy with plenty of batteries. Because banks and ATMs may be closed for a time after a hurricane, make sure to have cash as well. And remind your parents to fill your car with gasoline.

DURING A HURRICANE: Stay indoors. Low-lying areas may flood quickly and strong winds can blow things around. If you live in a mobile home, go to a shelter. If your home isn't on higher ground, go to a shelter. If emergency managers say to evacuate, do it right away.

AFTER A HURRICANE: Stay indoors until it is safe to come out. There can still be flooding even though the hurricane has ended. Many times there are snakes and balls of fire ants moving through the flood. Stay away from standing water because downed power lines may cause the water to be electrically charged. It's also important to wait until officials say it is safe before drinking tap water.

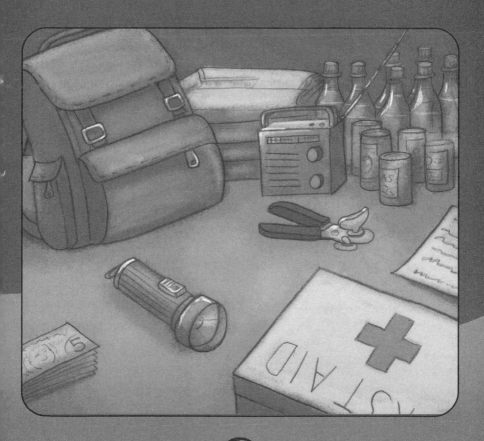

The Saffir-Simpson Hurricane Scale

Like the Fujita Tornado Intensity Scale, there is a scale for hurricanes. It is the Saffir-Simpson hurricane scale. Here are how hurricanes are rated:

Tropical Storm — Winds 39 to 73 mph (62 to 117 km/h)

Category 1 Hurricane — Winds 74 to 95 mph (119 to 153 km/h) No real damage to buildings. Some damage to unanchored mobile homes and poorly constructed signs. Also, some coastal flooding and minor pier damage.

Category 2 Hurricane — Winds 96 to 110 mph (155 to 177 km/h) Some damage to roofs, doors, and windows. Considerable damage to mobile homes. Flooding damages piers. Small crafts may break their moorings. Some trees blown down.

Category 3 Hurricane — Winds 111 to 130 mph (179 to 209 km/h) Some structural damage to small buildings. Large trees blown down. Mobile homes and poorly built signs destroyed. Flooding near the coast destroys smaller structures with larger structures damaged by floating debris. Terrain may be flooded well inland.

Category 4 Hurricane — Winds 131 to 155 mph (211 to 250 km/h) More extensive curtain wall failures with some complete roof structure failure on small residences. Major erosion of beach areas. Terrain may be flooded well inland.

Category 5 Hurricane — Winds 156 mph and up (251 km/h) Complete roof failure on many residences and industrial buildings. Some complete small buildings blown over or away. Flooding causes major damage to lower floors of all structures near the shoreline. Massive evacuation of residential areas may be required.